DRAW IT!
COLOR IT!
CREATURES

HOUGHTON MIFFLIN HARCOURT

Boston   New York

Go on, add some teeth.
I dare you!

Axel Scheffler

HAMISH the Hairy Dog

(just add hair)

MY
RARE BUTTERFLY
COLLECTION

RARE BUTTERFLY no. 1

RARE BUTTERFLY no. 2

RARE BUTTERFLY no. 3

Four of the
most unusual
butterflies in
the world.

YOU
can make
it happen!

RARE BUTTERFLY no. 4

Find all 6 fish and
color them in!

Squirrel wears a wig.

Duck wears a hat.

What will you draw for Penguin and Cat?

An armchair, a bike, and a very old telly.

What else has this hungry whale got in her belly?

Rob Biddulph

Bear can't leave until the train is full!

Can you help him fill each carriage?

Birgitta Sif

Draw their dreams . . .

Heavy snowstorm! Draw the penguins in caps and scarves! Add extra penguins too, for warmth!

SUSANNE GöHLICH

This little beast is having a feast!

Can you draw his picnic?

Draw his picnic pal!

Sara Ogilvie

Draw the dragon's fiery flames . . .

Draw the other monster in the
monster battle!

Alexis Deacon

Who's making all that noise?

YOU decide.

ROAR!

tim hopgood

Who lives in this house?

Who is driving

these cars?

EKATERINA
TRUKHAN

Can you draw the other half to make a full creature?

Tor Freeman

HUNGRY BUGS AND INSECTS

are eating

all my plants . . .

Leave some for me!

David Mackintosh

What's the pigeon looking at?

Give him some friends and

fill the tree with golden leaves.

JIM FIELD

DRAW the weirdest creature
you have EVER seen.

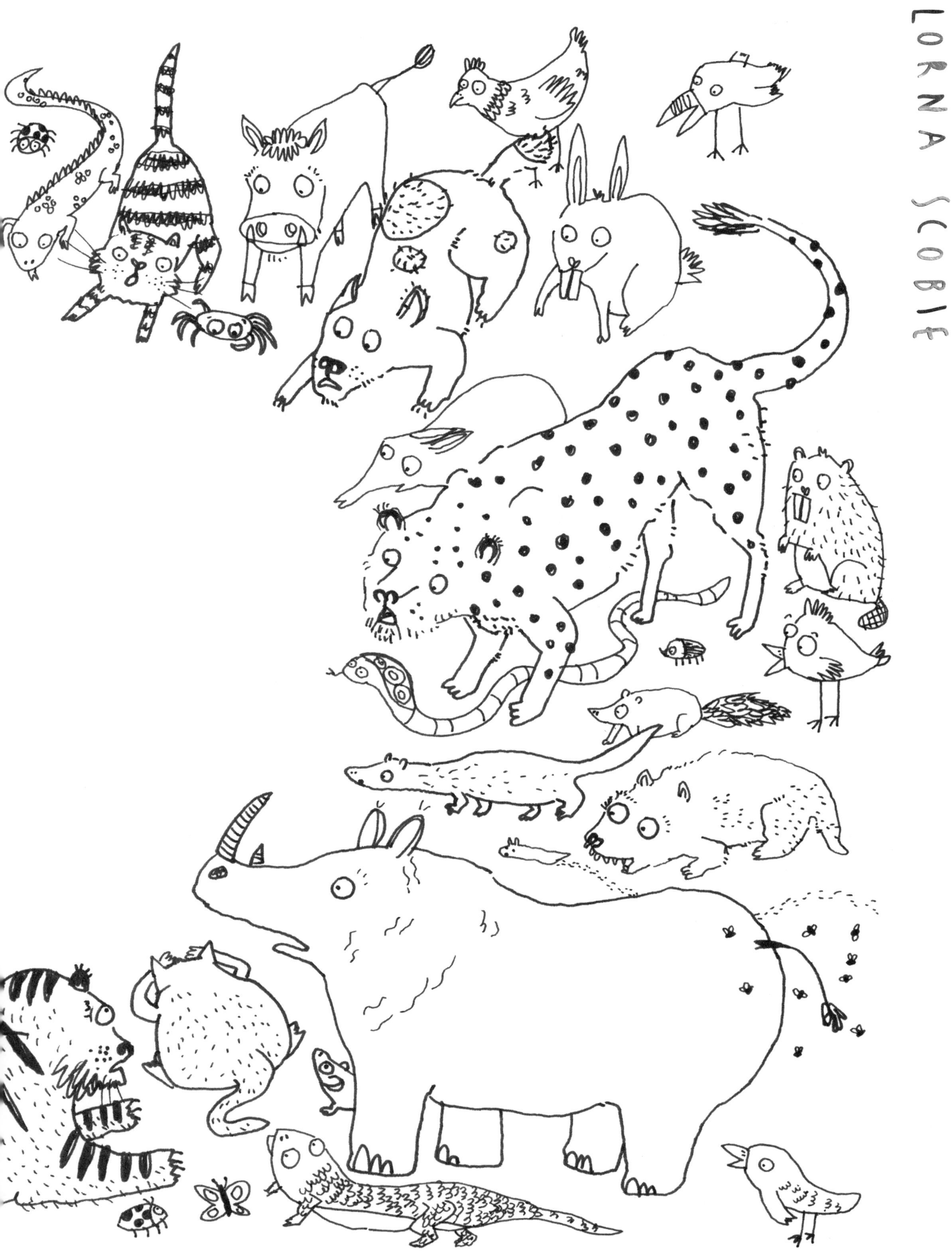
LORNA SCOBIE

Will someone join me for a drink?

Benjamin Chaud

What other creatures
live in the tree?

Briony May Smith

Oh, no! He's being eaten alive! But what by?

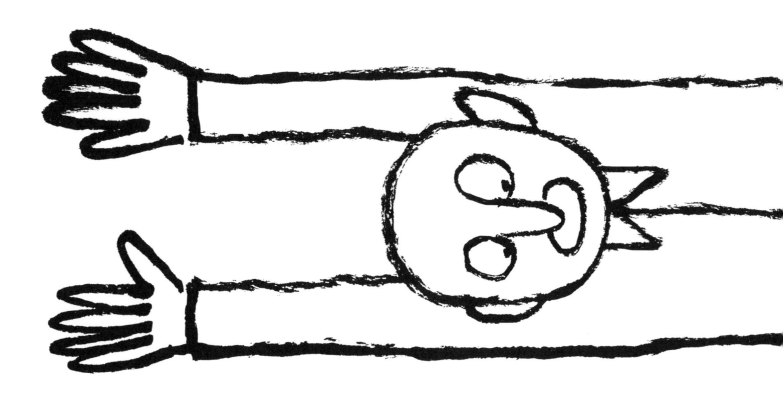

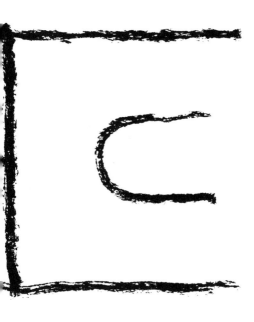

Can you help and make

the sheep woolly and warm?

Britta Teckentrop

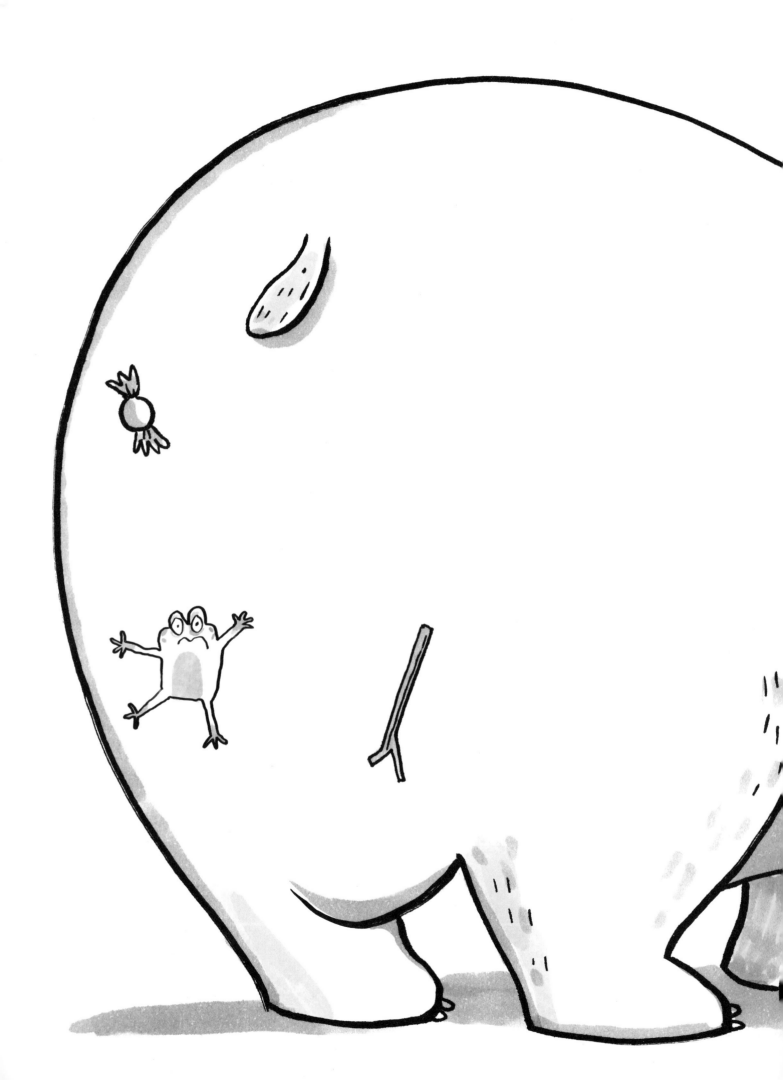

Draw what's stuck to bear's bum!

Nikki Dyson.

What does the baby alien's spaceship look like?!

Rebecca
Patterson

What a lot of rubbish! Can you transform this rubbish into fun creatures?

Could this be a rabbit?

A dinosaur or a bird?

A monster?

Have
fun!

Zehra Hicks

Make this a dog!

Make this a cat!

Yasmeen Ismail

Who is this bear hugging?

The three-headed beast is missing two heads!

Can you help?

BARBARA NASCIMBENI

Whose shoes?

Can you draw the rest?

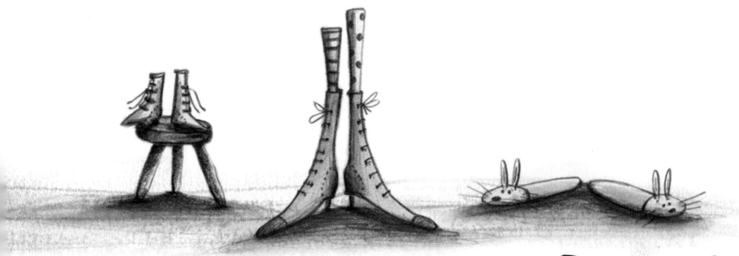

BIRGITTA SIF

TWO
MONSTERS
(or possibly more . . .)

Chris Riddell

Draw more fish for this mermaid to photograph.

marta altés

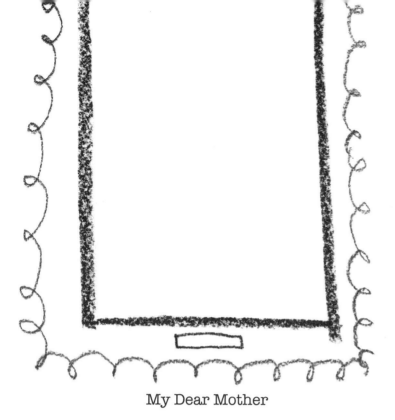
My Dear Mother

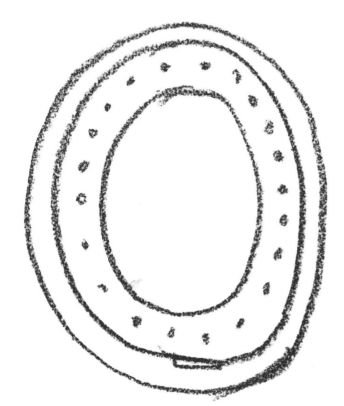
School Principal

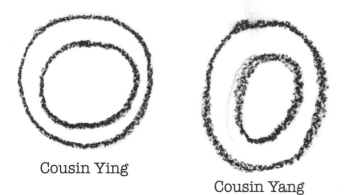
Cousin Ying

Cousin Yang

MEET
MY
FAMILY

and OTHER
CREATURES

Half-Brother Mike

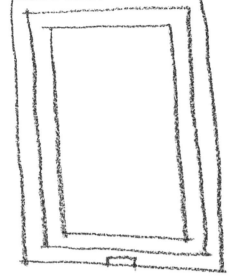

Uncle Xark

David Mackintosh

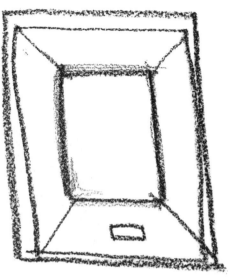

My Sister Pearl

Grandma Jeremy

Cousin
Bradley

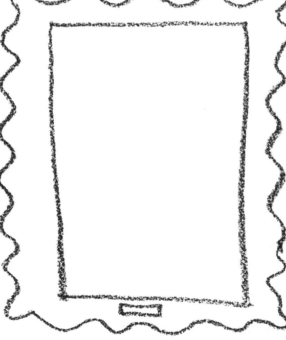

Dear Father

Captain Sergeant,
My Nanny

Auntie Penny

Aunt Melanie

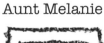

Little Minky

My First Pet,
Martin

Color me in, please.

(Can you make my tail wag too?)

Uh-oh, this painter is NOT paying attention and this lady is furious! She's covered in paint! Can you draw her?

JIM FIELD

They're all VERY hungry . . .

But what will

they eat?

A posse of peacocks—
I think I count nine.

Brighten each tail
with its own
cool design.

What does this airship look like?

Kazuno Kohara

Sarah McIntyre shows you

HOW TO DRAW A BIRD

with a real feather!

You will need:
* a feather
* a sharp knife & cutting board
(and an adult to help)
* ink
* paper
* paper towel for blotting

Lay feather on
cutting board

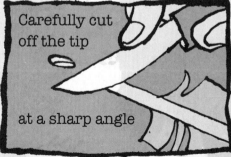

Carefully cut
off the tip

at a sharp angle

Now you have a
pointy tip!

If your nib breaks or dulls, just cut it farther up the shaft of the feather!

Here's one easy way to draw a bird with your quill pen:

NOW YOU TRY!

CAT

↓

DOG

↓

MOUSE

↓

Russell Ayto

Can you draw Cat's space rocket?

Natalie Russell

Spots or stripes?

You decide!

Britta Teckentrup

This floor looks very empty! Shall we fill it up?

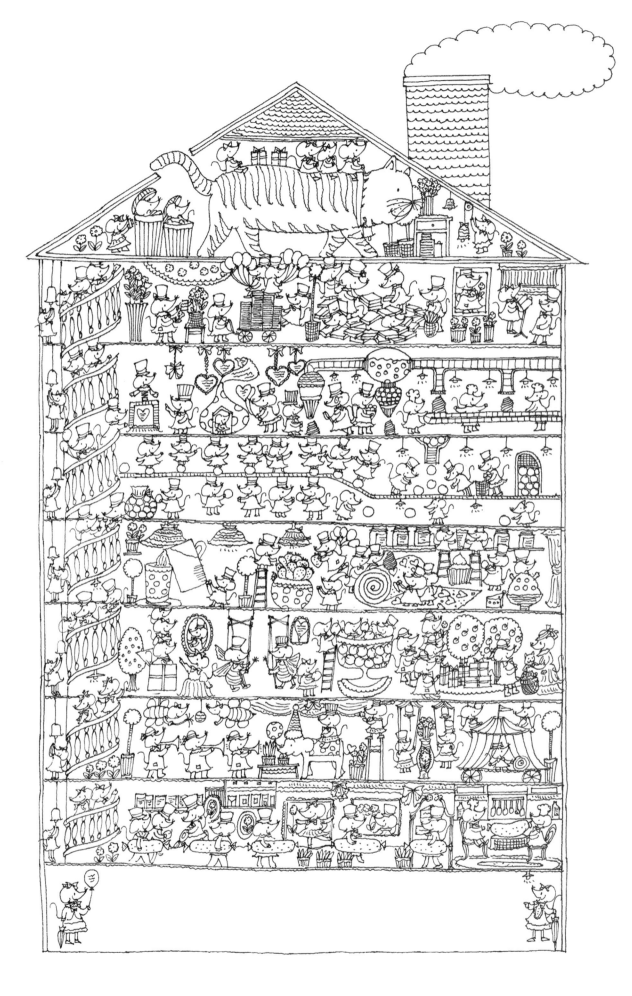

What do you think is happening on this floor?

Give him a lady!

Sven Nordqvist

COLOR THE BUGS!

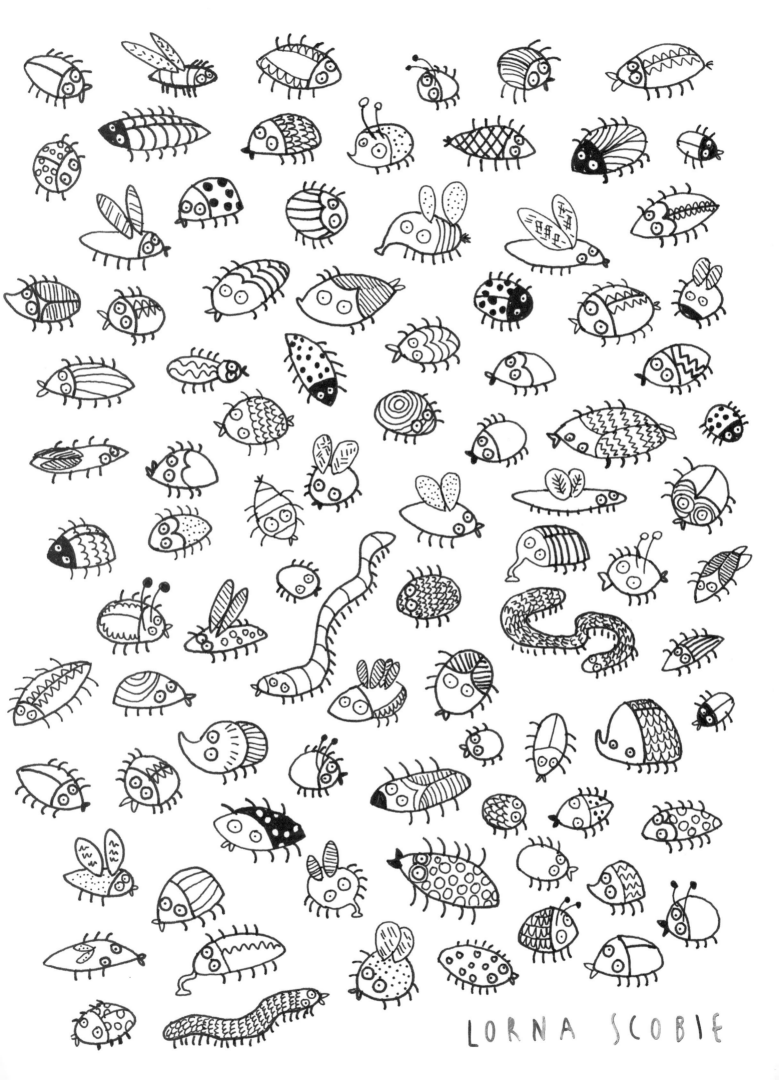

LORNA SCOBIE

Adam Stower

Granny has an interesting new pet. What is it?

Gosh! That's a snazzy cardigan!

Who, or what, is wearing it?

Alex T. Smith

Make me a
colorful cat!

Matt Spink

This beast likes to BOOGIE.

Can you draw his dancing buddy?

Sara Ogilvie

Draw the creatures that live in these houses . . .

Alexis Deacon

Draw the birds!

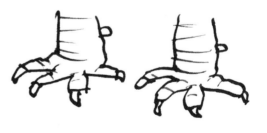

Sven Nordqvist

The Teddy Bears' Picnic!

Can you draw some food in the bears' bellies,

some leaves on the trees, owls in the hollows,

spots on the mushrooms, and flowers on the stalks?

Emily MacKenzie

It's the Monster Ball tonight.

These customers would like a fancy hairdo!

Jools Bentley

Color in these creatures.

Now turn these shapes into something fun!

Benji Davies

Poor Stephen—what has

he been eating?

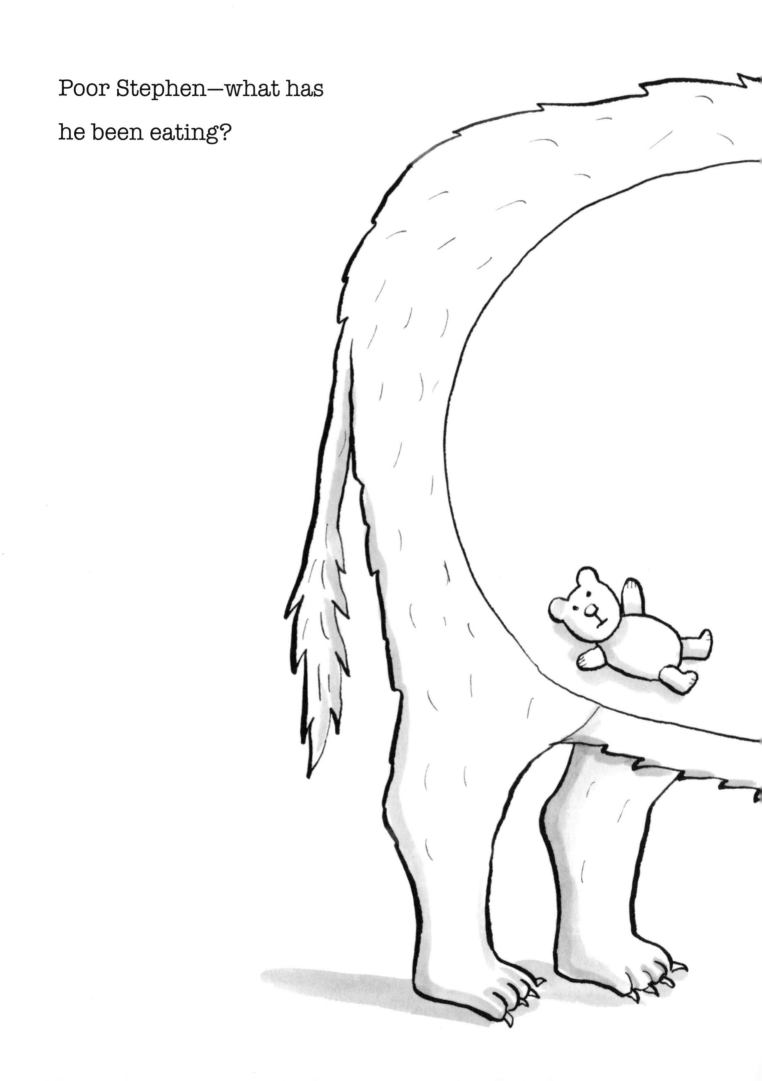

Axel Scheffler

Birds in frocks
and socks . . .

chris
Riddell

followed by a bear
in a cheesy hat,
bauble mittens,
jingle bell coat, and
snuggly slippers . . .

followed by . . .

Create and color creatures!

Kitty Crowther

These giraffes need some patterns.

Emma Carlisle

Special creature delivery!

Draw a baby creature being carried in the stork's cloth bundle.